THOMAS & FRIENDS

The Big Job

In these stories you will meet:

Harvey

Percy

Bertie

Rocky

Gordon

Edward

And this  crane

EGMONT

We bring stories to life

Book Band: Yellow

First published in Great Britain in 2016 by Egmont UK Limited,
The Yellow Building, 1 Nicholas Road, London W11 4AN

Thomas the Tank Engine & Friends™

CREATED BY BRITT ALLCROFT

HiT entertainment

ISBN 978 1 4052 8259 8

63403/1

Printed in Singapore

Stay safe online. Egmont is not responsible
for content hosted by third parties.

Series and book banding consultant: Nikki Gamble

FSC MIX Paper FSC® C018306

The Big Job

This is Rocky.
He is a big crane.

Gordon, Edward and Thomas did not want Rocky.

He is too big.
We do not
need him.

7

Rocky wanted to help Edward.

Edward did not want
Rocky to help.

But then Edward
had a bump.

Edward got Harvey to help.
But it was too hard
for Harvey.

Crash!
Now Gordon
needed help, too.

Edward got Rocky.

Rocky was
happy to help.

Now Gordon, Edward and Thomas do want Rocky.

He is big and we need him!

Crash!

This is Harvey.
He is a crane.

Harvey was sad
to hear that.

33

Then Percy had a bad day.

Stop, trucks! Stop!

Crash went Percy
and the trucks.

Percy was stuck.

Bertie the Bus was stuck.

Harvey was happy to help.

Big Crash!

These two pictures of Percy crashing look the same but there are five differences in the second picture.

Can you find them all?

Answers: Percy's face has changed and his number is missing, one sheep is missing, the sign above the bridge is not there and the far wall of the bridge has gone.

Read these words:

crash   bash   smash

Harvey the Crane

Which of these words best describe Harvey?

good   bad   crane   train